Shorts and Thoughts

Maggie Fogarty

Thanks to my husband Paul who has helped with the formatting of this compilation and has been a good sounding board. Also to Spencer Smart for his work on the cover and my website. Last but not least to Bonnie dog, the cheeky cockapoo, who keeps us on our toes and never tires of walkies on our local beach.

Alan and Barbara - A Life in Fives

It was Billie Holiday's voice that did it.

'You Go To My Head' was the song and that's exactly what Barbara did that evening. She's stayed there ever since too, though I much prefer heart rather than head.

Let me set the scene. Gino's Cafe, just off High Street, in Falmouth. The place was a lot less trendy back then, more hippy than hipster. It was a day in May and the date contained all of the fives – 5/5/1965.

Me, the gauche art student, dressed soberly in a black polo neck jumper with an unfashionable musical fixation with jazz. Billie Holiday winning over the Beatles every time.

'Babs' as she liked to be known, a vision in a red cotton mini dress with black patent sandals. Auburn hair styled in a trendy Twiggy short bob and those eyes. Green with distinctive brown flecks. The eyes dominated, twinkly, playful, intelligent. Framed by the palest of skins with a smattering of freckles on an upturned nose.

Perfect.

It was the end of the evening, me the only customer left. Eking out the dregs of my coffee and watching Babs as she tidied up behind the counter.

'OK for me to put on one last record?' I asked, fully expecting a 'sod off home' retort.

She didn't turn around but replied 'Go on then. Just the one mind.'

Sometimes I wonder what would have happened if she'd just said no. Funny how life can turn on a sixpence, to use an old money term. Heads you win... and that evening I won big time.

There were only two Billie tracks on the juke box and one was 'Strange Fruit'. Haunting and disturbing, but hardly a 'toe tapper' as my granny would say.

So it had to be the other one and it became a track of our lives.

At first Babs seemed oblivious to the song, stacking cups mechanically before running a soggy cloth over the counter. Then the pause, those incredible eyes staring into the distance, into a world far away from the end of day cleaning routine and a greasy cafe.

'That's a beautiful song...who is it?' she asked, finally blinking out of her reverie, absorbing the reality of the drab surroundings.

That's when I knew she'd got it. That she understood Billie, that voice of voices. Babs could appreciate what my art school friends scoffed at as 'old hat' and I fell in love on the spot.

As the saying goes, that was then and this is now. Half a century gone and we are still together of sorts. Babs and me.

Today is the fiftieth anniversary of our first meeting and with every passing decade we've marked the occasion. Of course there have been other celebrations - wedding anniversaries. the births of our two children, work promotions and Bab's graduation from the Open University.

But the day we first met has always been the 'special one', the catalyst for everything else that followed. This time around it's going to be a different kind of a celebration. Not jumping on a plane to somewhere warm like we used to, though I'd do anything to still be able do that. No, my idea is to recreate our very first meal out together in that long summer of 1965. Simple but effective and I know Babs will love it.

Way back then, 'Le Cep' bistro was tucked away off Church Street, the coolest place in a more shabby than chic Falmouth town and it was packed out that night. We didn't go for the fancy French stuff though, preferring a better cooked version of what we already knew. Steak, chips and peas. Washed down with a bottle of Claret and a small brandy to follow. Never has a meal tasted so delicious and trust me, we've had our fair share of gourmet food over the passing years.

Our talk was carefree and light, matching our mood. We kissed goodnight but that was it, me heading back to my grotty student digs after making sure Babs got her last bus home. My flat mates poked fun of course, expecting me to be out for the rest of the evening. This was the swinging 1960s after all, even in a Cornish dock town.

Still, the kiss was the start of something special and we both knew it...

To help me get in the mood for our latest celebration, I've dug out the photo the waiter took that night, me in my one and only smart striped jacket and Babs in her pale lemon lace dress, hair back combed and more bouffant than usual. We're smiling, our newly served meal still uneaten. The bottle of wine sitting inside a wicker basket holder, two large glasses already poured.

Snapped and suspended in time.

Right now Babs is staring across at me, the eyes unchanged over the years. An older but still beautiful version of herself.

'Darling, shall I put on some Billie while I prepare our dinner?'

No answer of course but I know she approves, that familiar look which I've never tired of, saying it all.

Some music and wine then before the preparations begin. The first Billie track has to be the one that sealed our fate. The one that truly went to our heads, changing our lives forever.

I place a glass of wine in front of Babs and I swear there's a flicker of delight, the tiniest suggestion of a smile.

Isn't it strange how music can recreate memories and allow you to time travel at will?

In an instance, I'm back in the 1920s semi Babs and me bought when we got married, a little over a year after we first met. I'd just landed myself a reporter job on the local newspaper and Babs was already expecting our twins. One boy and a girl, 'a pregnancy of convenience' she had joked. Two for the price of one.

The tiny seaside town of Marazion was more sedate than Falmouth but we loved the place and never tired of the view across to St Michael's Mount, along with the beach snaking all the way down to Penzance. My old art school mate, Harry Golding, scoffed at my domesticity and new small town life.

'Alan what the hell happened to that guy who wanted to live in Paris and spend his days painting?' I can still see Harry perched on the kitchen table, eyeing up the place with a mix of disdain and terror of what might happen to him.

'Things change,' I replied not wanting to get into an argument. Truth is, it was the happiest I'd ever been. Hand on heart. Half a century later, Marazion is still home though the house is bigger with an even more stunning view across Mounts Bay.

Time now to season the steak and fashion some finely cut chips, or 'frites' as they called them in that tiny restaurant a life time ago. 'Frites and petit pois'. Back then we laughed at the pretension but it still felt incredible. A weekend wages sort of incredible, not that I ever let her know that.

Billie has moved on and is singing 'Summertime'. Another of our favourites, eh Babs?

The track is still running as I finish preparing the frites, all perfectly thin and blanched. A labour of love can't be rushed and Billie's languid voice is the finest of backdrops.

There's my hand written letter to Babs, lying on the kitchen table. It's been our little tradition and I've written one to mark every passing decade of our lives together. Each still survives, carefully stored in an old tin box which Babs has customised with hand drawn hearts, flowers and those silly smiley faces that she always loved to draw on steamy windows.

'Are you ready for me to read my darling?'

Our letter ritual has stayed the same and if you'd told me back in 1965 that I'd still be writing those declarations of love and respect, I'd never have believed you. Like every 20 something, I couldn't imagine getting to my eighth decade. When the Beatles sang about being 64, it was a bit like those tops of mountains, shrouded in mist. You knew the summit was out there somewhere, way out of sight, just like old age is to the younger generation.

My hand writing is 'lousy' to quote Babs. Blame it on the short hand and all those hours spent as a court reporter. I swear I had a neater hand before becoming a journalist but then again, it's the words that count. Here we go, are you listening Babs? Those eyes stare back, full of expectation.

'Darling Babs,

Well my love, here we are on the fifth decade of our meeting, half a century flying by. Slowly to begin with, then with a scary acceleration. Is that what growing older is really all about – each year passing with increasing speed? I remember when we joked about the significance of that fifth of May in year five of the 1960s. Was the number an omen?

Now we've come full circle to that little number and in keeping with the theme, I'm going to write down five things I want to celebrate about our lives together.

The first has to be our love which never diminished, growing in strength as the years have passed. Of course there was lust too – those early long weekends where we barely got out of bed – but it was always much more than that. I know you felt the same and our sort of love was never going to go out of fashion or be traded in for a newer model. A bit like Billie Holiday's voice, we were always meant for the long haul.

A pause for a sip of wine. I swear I can see her eyes misting over. Or is that me I'm describing?

'Then our beautiful twins, James and Kate, who couldn't be better kids. You were a fantastic mother, always there when I was climbing the slimy newspaper pole, sometimes too enthusiastically. When I finally managed to slide back down, they were all grown up and off on their own life adventures. We always knew Kate

would be a doctor but James kept us guessing, finally growing into the fine artist I once hoped I'd be. Kate will be here soon and as usual she'll tell her dad off for drinking too much. Can you really have too much wine at this age Babs?

Talking of vino, there's another vintage bottle of finest red still untouched. We bought a whole case of them on our first 'meeting day' anniversary, promising only to drink one every ten years and here it is, waiting to be opened with our special meal. Food has always been such a glorious part of our lives, eaten in some splendid places across the world and in our very own Cornwall. Who'd have thought this part of England would become such a culinary delight with brilliant places popping up everywhere? While we could never agree on the best local food – you Padstow, me St Ives – we managed to sample plenty of those gourmet delicacies. You were always a brilliant planner Babs, cutting through my excuses and procrastination and making sure we ticked off those dishes.

When you finally graduated at the age of 46, no one could have been more proud. You were far brighter than you'd been led to believe by those too stupid to appreciate your true talent. And to think you thought you were old back then, questioning whether it might be too late to take up study. Of course it wasn't and it was fantastic to watch you grow in confidence, becoming a first class teacher. You showed them my Dr Barbara, crashing through their barriers and entering that world beyond.

And now the fifth and final celebration...'

A pause, a need to move closer, to touch that face.

My fingers slide across the icy glass of the photograph frame, your image frozen in time. It was taken on that last holiday in the Scilly Isles, just eight months ago, the sun catching your hair and mirrored in those sparkly eyes.

Little did we know then what lay ahead, how illness had already invaded your body and would take on its vicious final grip.

Must keep things together now Babs. It's just how you would have wanted it, celebratory and joyous, smiles not tears.

'My love, here's to that day we first met. When you went to my head and will never ever leave. Wherever else you are now, you are still here with me, laughing, crying, telling me off for not sorting out my paperwork. Those little but still big things, the stuff of growing old together.

To us – Alan and Babs.

And to Billie of course, whose voice made our magic happen.

In that wonderful Spring of fives.

Key

The remnants of our last game of Scrabble are scattered across the floor. Disconnected letters, strewn and jumbled with the play board dangling off the window sill.

What is it doing there?

My eyes flick back to the pile of plastic letters. In the chaos I spot the word 'key'. I smile at this small discovery of order in disorder, a little word with a pleasing score. Result.

Then the scream. A deep primitive sound that erupts from who knows where. Almost two decades later, I can recreate every piercing note. Pitch perfect.

Today I stare at the faded front door from my vantage spot at the bottom of the hallway stairs. Everything is so much smaller than I remember, the walls closing in around my now adult body. I helped paint that door, mum scolding me for getting splashes on her new apricot carpet. The carpet is long gone, replaced by functional tiles but for some reason the door hasn't been touched in all these years.

I feel compelled to run my fingers across the paintwork, a physical connection with my childhood. Raised rivulets of dried paint, a reminder of that scorching hot summer. The last of my carefree days, though little did I now that then. . .

'Stop using so much paint - it dries quickly in this heat.'

Mum in denim shorts and pink shirt, her sheer lip gloss glinting in the sunshine. She was never without make-up, her 'war paint' as she called it.

I freeze as the letter box opens stiffly, spewing out leaflets for pizza deals and furniture sales. Then the official looking brown envelope poking out from the heap of garish flyers, the one I've been waiting for. A glance at the spidery handwriting tells me all I need to know.

So he's got back then. Replied to my letter, the first in over twenty years. It's not as though he hasn't tried to make contact. In the early days, after he went away, there were loads of letters. I just ignored them, hoping that he'd stop and disappear from my life. After a while he did just that - until now.

The writing is tiny and squashed like the house. He's leaned hard on the pen and there's an inky puncture where my name starts. I wonder what he thinks about me being back here, the place where all our lives were shattered. How does that song go? 'What a difference a day makes.'

Well you can say that again. Dad.

The envelope tears open easily, a thin cheap thing. The paper inside has been wrenched from a note pad, the frayed edges roughly folded over. I get a whiff of cigarette smoke and something else. Ginger or Cinnamon? I'm not sure which. A hint of aftershave perhaps - like the ones mum would buy him for birthdays and Christmas. Dad used to go big on those man perfumes, laughing when I held my nose.

'Ugh dad, you stink'.

He'd chase me around the house before lifting me and burying my face in his chin. I'd giggle, squirming against the mix of stubble and the acrid stench of whatever mum had bought him this time around. Stinky he may have been but he was still my dad, mischievous and full of fun.

Right then, here goes. Let's see what he has to say after all this time, what he thinks of my plan. I can't believe how much my hand is shaking, how the sight of his writing has propelled me straight back to the 10 year old girl I was when I last saw him.

'Dear Sarah,

Your letter came as a shock but what a wonderful one. At last my prayers have been answered and can't imagine how overjoyed I am to hear from you. I never gave up hope that one day you'd get in touch and of course I want to meet you. There is so much to say and to explain now that you are grown up. I hope that in time you'll come to understand what happened and what caused me to do what I did. I don't expect forgiveness but will try to explain the chaos, the volcano that was in my head back then. You say that you have returned to our old house and have bought it. That I find hard to understand and why you want us to meet there. I'd be happy to travel over to Warwick even though I'd barely recognise the place today but there are so many memories, such trauma and darkness in that house. If you insist, of course I will have to steel myself to do it. So please let me know exactly when you want us to meet.

Much love,

Dad x

PS: I understand why you don't want to give a telephone contact but can we at least email?

After reading the letter several times, I can feel myself getting more irritated. I'm not sure what I expected but it wasn't this. His line about explaining things 'now that you are grown up'. As for suggesting a different place to meet, that's him all over, the need to control. Well this little visit will be at my place and on my conditions. He isn't having another way to contact me either. Only by letter and at this address.

I try telling myself not to let his words get to me, that it's me in the driving seat today. After all I've already taken the biggest step in buying my old family home, the thing he finds the most difficult to understand. Admittedly, not many people would come back to a house that has a history of so much pain and sorrow. But I find it strangely comforting, cathartic even.

When the estate agent showed me around, he said nothing about past events here. Perhaps he didn't know as he enthused over the 'spacious living room' and '1930s bay windows.' I recall how his words washed over me as the past crashed wildly into the present. I could picture myself in my school uniform, confused by the silence and that misplaced scrabble board.

'Mum – what's with all this mess? Where are you?'

My slow walk into the living room, the very one the estate agent is now talking up. Then that image, the one that has never left me. Mum sprawled across the new cream settee, her mouth wide open, eyes staring. Chillingly still. The scream, my panicked phone call to dad and not able to get hold of him. The run across our neighbour Mrs Roberts – I never knew her first name – and the shrieking sound of sirens. Mrs Roberts giving me a mug of hot chocolate.

'Don't worry your dad will be here soon.' The first of many lies.

'So what do you think of the house so far?' The estate agent's voice cuts in, catapulting me straight back into the present. I mumble something about wanting to view upstairs and thinking that if he could only see the images in my head, he'd run a mile.

I put in an offer on the house that day and once again it's my home, even though it bears little resemblance to the one I knew. The previous owners gutted the place, probably hoping that new paint and paper would obliterate the past. Inner walls have disappeared and there's a bright new conservatory at the back.

All change except for that front door, the one I'm still staring at.

After the day that rocked my world, the little childhood I had left was spent in Wales with my auntie Maureen. A plumper version of my mum, there was just three years between them in age. Strange how we rarely talked about what had happened. When his letters arrived they went unread, straight onto Maureen's coal fire. Sometimes I overheard her whispering about 'a row that got out of hand' and that 'he always had a temper that one.' Truth is I never saw any of that. If mum and dad argued, they hid it from me. I don't remember much affection between them either but they sort of just coasted along, my folks pure and simple.

It is often said that people study psychology to make sense of themselves and others. To explore how they fit into the great scheme of things and striving for order from chaos. A bit like those games of Scrabble I used to love, building words out of a muddle of letters.

Over time I changed my surname to mum's maiden one, Clarkson, and now everyone knows me as Dr Sarah Clarkson, psychologist. I don't avoid the hard cases either, far from it. If anything my background gives me more of an insight, better knowledge if you like.

So dad, how to reply? Short and sweet I think. A date and time, no procrastination or negotiation.

....

June 15, just before 3.00pm and here I am waiting, sitting childlike on my stairwell. He's due any minute and I suspect he'll be on time. I've rehearsed what I'm going to say and have calmed myself with Yogic breathing.

Then the doorbell, a single sharp press. Another deep breath before I open the door.

A gaunt man stands before me and I'm struggling to recognise who it is. Until I see the eyes, shrunken and hooded but undeniably his.

Already his hand is out stretched.

'Sarah – you look so...'

He's lost for words but I don't help him. I spot small tears forming at the corner of his eyes as he struggles to speak.

'Beautiful. Tall too...'

I made sure I put on my highest heels, not expecting him to be so small. In my memory he is the big one, towering and muscular.

A seemingly long pause as I stand over him, staring and silent.

When my voice comes, I try to sound calm,

controlled. Dr Sarah, the professional.

'Come inside, it doesn't look anything like our old house.'

He hesitates, reluctant to remove his eyes from me and to step over the threshold.

'Do we really have to talk here? Can't we go somewhere else – please?'

I meet his gaze for longer than is comfortable.

'No, here is where it has to be.'

He puts his arm out again and this time I take it, shocked by the thinness. I guide him into the hallway and his eyes go straight across to the living room. It's bigger now, reshaped.

He's taking his time, drinking in the scene, confused by the changes.

I can see that he's staring at the corner where our old settee stood, where mum was found.

'Sarah I don't think I can go back in there.'

Dr Clarkson straightens her back and looks down on him with a mix of pity and rage. This is her surgery and he's her patient. An appointment booked and arranged.

'Of course you can. I'm holding on to you. Come on, I want to hear everything you've got to say.'

I've positioned a picture of him, mum and me on the mantelpiece. It was taken six months before our world imploded and we're all smiling at the camera.

A happy family - or so it seemed on that day.

Catching sight of the photo, he flinches, pushing against my grip on his arm.

'Sarah please...'

I mirror the smile on my childhood photo as I steer him into the living room, my eyes fixed on mum.

'Go on, speak to mum. Explain what you did and I'll jot everything down.'

I'm still clinging on to him as I grab hold of my note pad. It's personalised with my full title on the front.

His eyes flit between me and the book.

'So you're a Dr then...what, you want me to talk like I'm one of your patients?'

I nod, my stare determined and guide him towards one of the high backed chairs I've put out especially for his visit. He sits on the edge of the seat, his hands gripping the sides as if his life depends on it.

He is sweating now, small beads of moisture forming along his receding greying hairline. I look back across at the image of mum, carefree and the picture of happiness. Then the younger him, about two stones heavier and with a thick mop of dark wavy hair.

'Take your time' I say, keeping my gaze firmly on mum. Mrs Janet Mason, nee Clarkson. Died aged

35, not that much older than I am today.

He shifts awkwardly, turning away from the family portrait and I can see that his eyes are watering. For a few seconds I feel sorry for him, this pathetic shell of the man I used to call dad. Then my professional persona kicks in, pen at the ready. When he finally begins, his voice is quivering, barely a whisper.

'I'd got back early that day after spending a few hours in the pub. I wanted some liquid courage to tell your mum about the row I'd had with the factory foreman that morning. I'd told him to stuff his bloody job and the low life sacked me on the spot.'

He coughs, and mutters an apology for his bad language. As if any of that matters.

'Go on' I reply, giving him another full on stare. He flinches and looks away.

'Well I got back here after pub chucking out time. Your mum was sat out in the garden reading a book, lost in her own little world. I asked her to make me a sandwich but she demanded to know why I was home at this hour of the day and 'stinking drunk' as she put it.

He swallows hard, focussing on my pen sweeping across the page.

'I don't really know why but suppose I just saw red. Years of pent up frustration about that crappy factory job and arsehole of a foreman. The contempt on Janet's face, a look of disgust and hatred. Next I remember dragging her into the kitchen shouting that all I wanted was a frigging sandwich.'

The tears are now cascading down his face, tracking the deep lines that have formed there over the years. I hand him a tissue which he takes and curls it into a tight ball. His hands are clenched, as if he is about to lash out.

I wait for a few minutes before prompting him to continue.

'She was crying, trying to cut slices of bread and calling me a useless string of piss. They were her words – *'useless string of piss.'* I grabbed the knife and she ran into the living room. She was screaming and bit into my arm trying to get me to drop the knife. All I remember then is the blood, her bumping into the table and the scrabble board hurtling across the room, stuff strewn everywhere. Then…'

His eyes move to the corner of the living room where mum was found. He looks like he's in a nightmarish trance, unable to move but forced to relive the events of that day.

'Then she just fell back on the sofa. There was a noise coming from her throat and I tried to get her to stand up. But she just went limp and the noise stopped.'

I can feel the tears pricking at my own eyes but he's too much in his own world to notice. My heart is thumping and my hands are clammy as I try to keep writing, to stay detached.

Everything he is saying has a familiar ring to it because in my time as a psychologist I've heard it all, over and over again. The trigger that starts everything off, the emotions heightened and stoked by alcohol or drugs, the final straw that snaps and the spiral into chaos. Lives ruined forever, love turned into violence and hatred. That red mist of extreme pain and rage.

This is text book stuff. Except it's my family, my mum and yes, my dad too.

Can the cycle of hate and anger ever be stopped? Can I begin to come to terms with the past and accept this pathetic looking man sitting in front of me as still my own flesh and blood?

For once in my professional life I don't have the answer, the pat solution. Sarah, the psychologist, is stumped for words. And for the first time in years I'm shedding tears for my mum, a ten year old girl in an adult body. Finally confronting the past - or at least one version of it.

All the while mum keeps smiling out from the photograph, forever young and glamorous. Exactly how I need and want to remember her.

Then reaching deep into my pocket, I seek out those three little scrabble letters I've carried around with me until this day.

My fingers trace out the word. K-E-Y.

Under my breath I whisper it.

'Key'.

The door to my troubled past is now ajar, neither fully opened nor closed.

So which is it to be?

In my heart I know the answer, though my professional brain is still unsure.

I've let him back through the door and in reality there is no going back. Forgiveness is quite another thing and it is too early to think about that.

For now it is all about evidence gathering, trying to understand, to put the pieces together.

'Sarah – I can see you are upset.' His words cut in, disarming me, a rare slip of the Dr Clarkson mask.

'No carry on. I need to hear this.' My reply is curt, disguising the turmoil inside.

He reaches across but I push him away.

This is going to take some time and there will be as many sessions as I think he needs. That I require too.

'Key'.

A device for opening and closing.

Tell Auntie

Pamela has a legion of fans and boy does she know it.

Her show on Cornwall's 'Go West Radio' has more regular listeners than any other. A mix of popular music and problem solving, a soothing voice and always her trade-mark sign off.

'Well that's it folks until next week. If you've got a problem you know what to do – I'm always here with a sympathetic ear.'

It's a privilege to be Pamela's producer, well her 'bit of everything' really. Friend, colleague, sounding board, runner and supplier of her favourite biscuits – chocolate bourbons with the occasional custard cream to ring in the changes. Always a cup of strong coffee, one sugar cube, the tiniest splash of milk.

Showtime for us is 8pm every Sunday. A time when everyone is preparing to face Monday, whether it be for work or just the start of another busy week. If you can believe all those lifestyle surveys, it is the point when anxiety starts to creep in, the weekend receding and challenges looming ahead. Perfect for a problem solving slot, or 'Agony Aunt' show if you want to be old school.

And boy is Pamela old school, stuck firmly in those carefree days before social media and the internet. When she first started work in back the 1960s, she was a secretary with speedy shorthand and fingers that flew across a typewriter like a concert pianist. That's her description by the way, which she often demonstrates on the old Silver Reed typewriter sitting defiantly at the back of the studio, surrounded by all the hi-tech radio gizmos.

'Good exercise for the old fingers' she tells me, although hers are now crooked from arthritis, her painted nails bent at different angles, an emerald cocktail ring dangling loose on the third right hand digit.

Pamela loves her pre-studio recording routines. Always coffee and a biscuit, a quick chat through the problems we are about to feature on the show. A final run through of the music choices, (no inappropriate tracks to cause offence), before heading into Studio 1. Drinks and food are banned in there just in case the equipment gets damaged by spills or crumbs. Pamela still carries a packet of strong peppermints though, an emergency ration in case of the dreaded dry throat.

Then Pamela takes to her throne behind the studio desk, a favourite cushion for back support, never finding the buttons and lights intimidating, despite her loathing of new technology and all things digital.

'This is just like a car,' she tells me 'ready to be driven. I'm at the wheel, in control and you know how much I love driving Lucille.'

Pamela steadfastly refuses to use my preferred shortened name, Lucy. No point trying to change things, been there and done that to no avail.

Then a quick glance in her compact mirror, making sure that that her make-up is just so. 'Always try to look your best, even on a radio show' is her mantra – something I choose to ignore, with comfort and warmth coming first.

Then we are off. Two hours of problems, told to Pamela as if she is their best friend, a trusted confidante.

First up is Maureen, with a broad Black Country twang despite having spent the past thirty years in Cornwall.

'The thing is Pam – er sorry Pamela – I'm at my wits end. He won't speak to my son and now we can't even see the grand children.'

I can see Pamela wincing at the voice on the end of the phone, the nasal Midlands accent being her least favourite. When she replies you would never know it, her voice lowered to convey sympathy.

'Oh you poor darling, caught between two warring males. Now my dear you need to put your foot down. Firmly mind. Insist on your right to see those lovely grand children.'

Maureen has started to sniffle, not uncommon on this show. In fact Pamela thinks she hasn't done her job properly unless there are at least two tearful outbreaks. She is well practised on which buttons to push,

'I know Pamela, you're right there chuck, but I can't force them to talk. Every time I mention it to my hubby, he just goes into a sulk for days. It's driving me mad and I haven't slept well for weeks.' A tearful pause, timed to perfection by Pamela.

'OK Maureen, this is what you need to do. You and your daughter-in-law must join forces and put those wise women heads together. Arrange to meet up for a girly weekend and think of a way of sorting this out. I'm sure those grand kids miss visiting their nanny in Cornwall.'

The mention of grand children sparks more tears, Pamela raising her eyes to the ceiling as she allows for another strategic pause.

Maureen blows her nose causing Pamela to wince and adjust her headphones. It's clear she wants Maureen off the line and soon.

'Just one thing before I go Pamela. I think I should mention that my son and daughter-in-law are going through a rough patch themselves, thinking of splitting up in fact.'

This sometimes happens. One problem leading to another and at this rate the call could go on for hours. Time to move on, pronto.

'Oh sorry to hear that Maureen, families eh?'

Pamela has gone back to the dipped voice, still sounding professional and sympathetic but needing to find a way out.

She tells Maureen that she is going to hand her over to the producer – yours truly – to give out contact numbers for family liaison professionals and the like. My list is at the ready and Pamela puts on a music track while I head back out into the office admin area.

'Lord that voice alone is enough to drive anyone up the wall' Pamela declares, as she prepares to move on to the next call.

Next up is Ian from nearby St Just. All calls are pre-screened so we know what is coming and can make sure there is a good spread of problems. At least that's the plan but as the saying goes, 'the best laid...'

His voice has changed from the genial but troubled young man I first spoke to a few days ago about his problem with loneliness.

'Pamela – I'm being straight up here, no flannel. I'm in serious trouble and need your help.'

The rules are clear. Anything criminal, a medical or mental health issue, can't be dealt with by us. Only everyday disputes and problems, the sort of things most of us experience as part of day-to-day living.

Pamela though is undaunted. She wants to hear a bit more before deciding to pull the plug.

'And what exactly is up Ian?'

Hopefully we can get him off quickly if he crosses a broadcast regulation line. Pamela nods across to me to show she is ready.

He coughs and then swallows hard.

'The thing is, my girlfriend is missing.'

Pamela moves forward, her twisted finger at the ready if the off switch is needed.

'Missing you say Ian...?'

Then what seems like a long pause, though it is only a few seconds.

'Yeah. Gone. Haven't heard from her since Wednesday night which has never happened before. The thing is...'

Another hesitation followed by a clear of his throat.

'What I mean is that something ain't right. Anything could have happened and she might even have been kidnapped, held against her will.'

Blimey, this is getting serious. Pamela needs to pull the plug and now.

'Kidnapped you say?' She ignores my gesture to go to some music, fast.

'Yeah cos there's no sign of her, no phone signal, nothing. I mean I know we had a bit to drink but that's not unusual for us...'

I'm leaning across the desk, trying to get to the

controls but Pamela is having none of it. What the hell has got into her? She knows the rules.

'Hmm. Take your time Ian. Just tell me what you can remember.'

Enough. I manage push the crucial button before Ian can say any more. We cut to an advertisement about double glazing while Pamela glares across, adjusting her ring as if it were a knuckle duster.

'What were you thinking of Pamela? Do you want us to lose our broadcast licence?'

Adjusting her microphone, she gives me another contemptuous look as the advertisement comes to an end.

'Sorry about that folks. We lost Ian but I'm sure like me, you are all worried about his girlfriend. We'll try to get him back but meantime here's another bit of music...'

My mobile phone rings out and it's Jeff, our station manager. He gives me an ear-bashing about the call, insisting that we don't put Ian back on the air.

Pamela's expression has now softened and she's scribbling something down. She looks nonplussed when I pass on the news from Jeff.

'Wouldn't it be great Lucille if we solved this? Find out where Ian's girlfriend is and reunite them?'

Still reeling from the Jeff call, I'm at a loss what to say but she's not giving up.

'Look Lucille. You have his number and we know he lives in St Just. If you phone him back we can get a few more clues, do a bit of digging.'

We're coming to the end of the music track and I have another person on the line wanting to talk about a dispute with a neighbour whose dog is barking constantly.

Pamela takes the call, and passes me the piece of paper she was writing on.

'Lucille, I want us to go and see this Ian guy at the end of the show.'

'Us'? This is getting out of hand, not like Pamela at all. We're radio workers, not private detectives. Come to think of it, we should really be calling the police, assuming they've not already got wind of Ian's call? And is 'Ian' even his real name?

What I should know about Pamela by now, is that she always gets her own way. No sooner has she signed off the show with her usual cheery words, than we are heading towards St Just in Pamela's vintage Alfa Romeo sports car, bright red with rusty pock marks scattered about like liver age spots.

'A bit like me' Pamela once quipped, patting the car as if it were a favourite pet.

We don't speak, Pam squinting in the darkness as she zips along the unlit winding road, me gripping the door hand rail, not wanting to distract her for fear of ending up on the other side of a hedge or granite wall.

As the street lights of St Just come into view, at last I can breathe properly.

'We'll park up in the Square and walk to the house' Pamela says, giving me a sideways glance. 'You all right Lucille? My driving isn't that bad.'

I ignore her, glancing down at my note of Ian's address. Assuming that it is his home, all we have is his word for it.

As if reading my mind – Pamela is good at that – she tells me to go with the flow, show some initiative and sense of adventure.

Easier said than done on a damp winter's evening in a town I barely ever set foot in. Still, the sooner we get this over with the better. Then back home to a nice glass of red wine and some re-heated left over chili con carne. Who says this gal doesn't know how to live? Sad I know, but right now that's exactly where I want to be.

The house isn't easy to find, tucked away behind the main street, one of a row of small terraced houses. Not many have visible numbers but eventually we manage to work out which is number 85. No lights on at the front, blinds shut tightly across the windows.

'Ring the phone number he gave you' Pamela orders, peering through the letter box.

Wanting to get this over as quickly as possible, I dial out and a phone rings on the other side of the chipped and dilapidated door. At least we're at the right place.

Tentative footsteps, a pause, then the voice.

'Hello...who is it?' He sounds wary, uneasy.

Yes, it's him all right, the same guy who phoned into the studio.

Pamela grabs my phone, giving me a thumbs-up.

'Ian? Is that you? It's Pamela here, standing right outside. Can I come in please?'

Silence. Water dripping from the overhead drain-pipe and bouncing off the pavement like an oversized teardrop.

Plop, plop, plop.

The door opens slowly, revealing a tall skinny young man, mop of red curly hair, quizzical brown eyes, the palest of skins, lips pinched.

'What are you doing here?' His voice has changed to a low hiss, eyes darting across the street to check if anyone is looking.

'Come on dear. Let us in. We're just here to help and this is Lucille by the way, you spoke to her earlier.'

We are ushered quickly into a dingy hallway, with frayed patterned carpet, the gagging smell of too many fried foods and cigarette smoke mixed with goodness knows what. If Pamela is as disgusted as me, she is doing a good job of hiding it.

He leads us into a tiny front room, dominated by a battered looking sofa, with discoloured yellowy foam filling protruding from the seats and arm rests.

'Sorry about the mess in here' he says, scooping up an ash-stray full of discarded cigarette butts. As if that will make any difference.

'My dear the mess in here is the least of your problems' Pamela says, sitting on the edge of the sofa, trying to get as little of it as possible in contact with her immaculate cream trench-coat. I opt to stay standing, a signal that we are not going to be here long. Just a quick check to see if he is all right and whether we have permission to pass on the details of his missing girlfriend to the police. That should do it.

Ian's face has morphed from one of concern about our arrival at the house to a grinning Pamela super fan.

'I can't believe you're here – wow, the real Pamela in the flesh.'

Pamela gives him a half smile, a mere flicker, and already I'm sensing there is something not right.

'Ian, shall we just talk about this missing girlfriend of yours?' Her voice is slightly higher than usual, a sure sign of stress.

He's squinting now, grin gone, tugging at his unruly red hair. I feel for my phone, deep at the bottom of my jacket pocket, loosening its protective cover just in case.

'You – close that door.' He jabs his finger close to my face, and I step backwards, the action achieving what he wants. A sudden click as it slams shut behind me.

'Now you sit down right there beside the lovely Pamela' he orders, gesticulating towards the grim sofa. Pamela shuffles sideways, giving me a reassuring look, one that says she'll handle this. It doesn't work and somehow I'll need to get to that emergency button on my phone.

He's breathing hard, eyes boring into the two of us, sensing our combined fear.

'Now Pamela, I've been doing a little bit of research on you. How you once found a missing girl, persuaded her to come back home. Am I right?'

This is news to me, not something that Pamela has ever mentioned.

'That was a long time ago Ian' she replies, taken aback by his question.

Phone pressing against my side, I inch closer to Pamela, her Lily Of The Valley perfume smelling stronger, pink blotch snaking across her neck, a mark of discomfort.

'So you can get my Amber back to me then?' His question is more of an order than a request.

Amber. Amber.

The name is ringing a loud bell and I can see that Pamela is thinking the same thing.

Amber, Amber...

Ah yes, now I remember.

The name of a young woman who contacted the show a week ago, asking for advice about a controlling and violent boyfriend. The one we spoke to off-air, referring her to a refuge, suggesting a way of escaping her terrible situation.

'Who exactly is Amber?' Pamela asks, trying to sound nonchalant, in control.

He's grimacing now, moving his face closer to Pamela. Cigarette smoke, a hint of garlic mixed with sweat, the underarms of his crumpled shirt dampened.

'You know damn well who Amber is. You sent her away from me, didn't you Pamela? So you'd better get her back, like you did with that other young girl.'

While he's fixated on Pamela, there's just about time to shift sideways, to push my hand into my pocket and feel around for the emergency button. A quick ping before moving back, swallowing hard to ease my dry throat.

Praying that I've pressed the right phone button and that it will work. Hoping too that our station manager, Jeff, will pick up a text message I sent to him just before we set off, giving him the address where we were heading and instructing him to alert someone if he hasn't heard back from me within the hour. Of course Pamela knows nothing of that message, and would have prevented me from sending it. It's my job to save her from herself and in this case, that could be literally.

Heart hammering, I'm hearing the story of Pamela's past rescue for the first time. A teenage daughter of her then boss went missing from boarding school back in the late 1960s. Pamela managing to track her down, persuading her to come home, her grateful boss telling a local paper what a fabulous employee she was. The seed of an idea about becoming a so-called 'Agony Aunt' sown right there,

'So Pamela, how are you going to fix this for me?'

This isn't a question but a threat, a demand that she puts right what Ian sees as a wrong. He took a punt on ringing into the station, a trigger to get Pamela interested. Bait, something to reel her in.

It's now been over an hour since I sent the text to Jeff and still no sign that the emergency phone button has worked. The combined smell of cigarettes, sweat and Pamela's sickly perfume, is making me feel lightheaded. Discreet wriggle of my toes to keep the blood flowing, a trick learned as a young naval cadet to prevent fainting during long times standing on parade.

Then we are thrust into the middle of a movie scene, with us at centre stage. Doors crashing, screams, Ian stopping mid rant, lurching backwards. He's shoved face down on the floor, cuffed, police officers mouthing the arrest warrant, Pamela and me ushered to one side for questioning.

Our radio boss Jeff, at first full of concern, then angry that we had put ourselves in danger by ignoring the health and safety rules of the station.

Oh, and no more Agony Aunt shows either, Pamela's reign of the airwaves is finished. Over and out.

For once Pamela stays quiet, letting Jeff sound off, agreeing that she should leave her beloved sports car parked in the Square and accept his offer of a lift home.

'Thank goodness Lucy had the good sense to alert me or heaven knows how this would have ended,' are his only words on the drive back.

The shock hasn't hit home yet, hyper arousal clinging on, the need for a strong drink. Forget the wine, only whisky will do it now.

Pamela is still rising above it all. Cool, regal, a smooth of her coat, slow twist of her cocktail ring.

Then the wink as she exits her car, whispering so Jeff can't hear. Fingers to her lips, head cocked to one side, ring stone glinting.

'Remember Lucille – I'm always here. See you next week.'

Then she's off, waving back at Jeff as if nothing untoward has happened. What a gal.

Somehow I know that Jeff will lose this battle royal with Pamela, he has no idea what he is up against.

Come to think of it, the same applies to me, the radio producer who thinks she has her presenter sussed. Yet in reality knows little, just mere glimpses, tiny giveaways.

The truth is, Pamela shows but never ever fully tells. That's just how she rolls.

Show time, every Sunday.

Auntie *really* does know best.

Random Pickings

It has to be the 11 bus. Always the 6am one because there are loads of empty seats and I can bag my favourite, on the far left hand side at the back.

This morning routine suits me fine, though I'm not travelling to anywhere in particular. I just love the steady motion, the stops and starts, the views into the houses below as the early risers start their day.

My route around the perimeter of the city takes a satisfying hour and a half. Enough to give me a glimpse of who does what and when, something to jot down in my note-pad, the one labelled 'YIPS' – an anagram for 'I Spy'.

You see, I really do 'spy with my little eye', my favourite travel game as a child. Yes me, the fifty something, still playing a kids game.

Hell Julie what are you thinking about?

It's the question I sometimes ask myself in those moments of self awareness which still creep in from time to time, along with those inner reprimands. Grow up. Take a grip. Get a life woman.

But this is my life, at least the first thing in the morning bit of it. It's part of who I am, the obsessive compulsive OCD Julie. The one I hide from my friends and family, the one I even managed to keep secret from my long term partner. Until last year that is, but more on that later.

Clarendon Road is my favourite on the route, long, with plenty of stops and a good mix of detached houses, shared properties and terraced homes.

Today, I've made a note to check in on number 10 and then the house further along the road which matches my age, 56. These have the longest entries in my note book, with lots of morning activities and they are both places where the occupants get up early.

A judder as the driver presses on the brakes and then the snake-like hiss as we pull into the first stop. The elderly man in number 10, a shabby red bricked terraced house with yellowing net curtains, is sipping his drink – I'm guessing tea – and thumbing through his morning paper, He's a real creature of habit is 'Mr T' as I call him.

'T' for 'tea' and also for 'ten'.

I like making links, it all adds to the game, and I've promised myself to look up his real name soon.

There are always a few people waiting to get on the bus outside his house, but I don't pay them much attention. It's 6.15 and Mr T is wearing the same jumper that he's had on all week. A dark blue cable knit one, with the left sleeve frayed. I've not seen any sign of another person in the house but he does have a ginger cat who I've called Baker – after the drummer Ginger Baker. No sign of Baker today though, but Mr T has left out some food for him, assuming of course that it is a 'he' cat.

'Morning – nice day isn't it?' Damn, one of the new passengers has decided that he wants to be friendly. Well he can go hang because I've got work to do. A curt nod from me does the trick and he scuttles off to the other side of the bus.

Back to Mr T then before we start to move off. He's sitting at the kitchen table as usual but seems distracted. Right now he's staring out of the window and I swear he just made eye contact with me. A fleeting quizzical glance, something to make a note of. That and the growing pile of washing-up in his sink. He's normally quite tidy so this is out of the ordinary, and there's another observation for me to record in bold letters.

'NO BAKER'.

A jolt and we are off. Time I think to take Mr T's observation to the next level. Get to know him better, worm my way into his life, to see where that journey takes me.

There are just two more stops before we get to house number 56, where there is an even longer snake of people waiting to get on. Today, one of the occupants of the smart 1930s semi detached house is sitting at her dressing table. The young woman who I've dubbed 'Annie Chestnut', to match the colour of her hair, is checking out her phone, her crowning glory hidden inside a large towel and she's still in her canary yellow night gown. She's running late today, as by now she is normally dressed for work in a uniform of black suit and crisp white blouse. Her boyfriend – somehow I think it is her boyfriend – is across the landing, his face reflected in the over sized mirror.

They are handsome couple, Annie Chestnut and 'Steve Stocky', with his sporty physique, tanned skin and curly blonde hair. Right in the middle of doing up their house, the lower front room has peeled away wallpaper and decorator cloths covering the floors. There's a ladder propped up against the hallway wall.

He glides across to the bedroom, mouthing something to Annie. She smiles then looks back at her phone, something more important grabbing her attention. Now he is staring straight ahead, a quick check of his watch.

God, can this be right? Is he about to set off for the bus? It's never happened before but it's looking that way, with another quick exchange of words between him and Annie. Then the perfunctory kiss before he heads straight out of the door, joining the back of the queue.

Heart hammering against my chest, a furtive shut of my note book, routine thrown out of the window.

What seems like a long wait, mouth feeling dry,

Will he sit close by?

He's tantalisingly near, heading for a seat just two rows ahead of me. Already he's opening his phone, just a sideways glance to check who is around. The middle-aged woman in the jogging outfit, sitting not far behind, isn't on his radar. By the way, that's me, the running clothes a good cover-up for my daily bus journey.

'Off on your usual run?' my neighbour had asked as I set off this morning.

As if.

Up close, Steve Stocky has touchable hair, a bit like those curly cross-breed dogs you see, the ones you want to ruffle.

Simultaneously tapping something into his phone, he shifts sideways as the bus starts to move, steadying himself against the rocky motion. Clearly someone who isn't used to this type of transport, slumming it for the day while his pristine convertible stays parked outside the house.

'Hi Kaz – how goes it?' His voice is more cultured than I imagined, a posh school sort, not quite the Jack-the-Lad bit of rough I'd guessed him to be.

Leaning forward, supposedly to adjust my trainers, I can just about make out the voice at the other end of the phone. It's a sing-song one, happy to hear from Steve.

'Yeah, let's grab coffee at that Greek Place and if you're lucky I might even treat you to breakfast. See you there in 5.' He's looking pleased with himself, the assignation sorted.

An audible giggle at the other end of the call, happy anticipation.

'That Greek Place'. I make a note and keep watch. Hell, I've got to go along with this, follow him when he gets off the bus.

Phone call finished, he's still staring down at the screen, no doubt scrolling through emails or social media.

Time to add to my note. *'Kaz. Wonder why? Will try to find out.'*

My eyes are still glued to him as he lifts his head up from whatever he is viewing on the phone. He makes a small adjustment to the top button of his jacket, a smart and expensive looking one. Keep them peeled Julie, he could be about to get off.

As the driver digs into the brakes, Steve Stocky is on his feet, grabbing the seat handle-bar. He's tall, over six foot, and his fingers are long, knuckles white with the effort of holding on.

I'll let him go first, hang back a little so as not to grab his attention. Allow another passenger go between us as we head down the narrow staircase, Steve treading carefully.

It's still quiet outside, only a few shops lit up, with smells of people making breakfast, a few raised voices ringing out, echoing off the almost deserted south Birmingham suburban pavements. Steve sets off at a brisk pace, with long no nonsense strides.

I can feel my breath growing heavier, trying to

keep up while still lagging suitably behind. This reminds me of my early police training in surveillance. Keep back, look natural, put on a hat to make you look different from the woman he might have glimpsed on the bus. Make out you are preoccupied with other things on the road. Once learned, never forgotten.

That life seems like an age away now. Me, the rookie police officer, patrolling the streets, with plans to be a crack detective. To specialise in undercover work yet being nudged towards child protection by my unreconstructed macho male boss.

The time before everything imploded, when my best friend and colleague lost his life, me left barely clinging on. Both of us attacked with knives which came from nowhere, him gone forever while I had no choice but to give up the job I loved.

Still, it has left me with skills, and to some extent PC Julie still exists and 'once a copper' as the saying goes. Back then to the target, Mr Steve Stocky, and already I can see the Greek Cafe ahead of him. I remember it well and it hasn't changed much since the early 1990s when this very road was one of my stomping grounds.

Never went in there back then. Can't say why, but the smells were always appealing, reminding me of carefree youthful holidays in Corfu, when the only things you had to think about were which bathing costumes to wear and where to go out for dinner.

Steve is heading inside, so time for me to hang back a little. Best cross over the road, keep walking straight on. Then double back after a suitable gap, by which time he'll be preoccupied by his companion. Fingers crossed.

Unlike the Greek Cafe, the road itself has been transformed over the decades. The houses are more spruced up – that's gentrification for you – and a lot of the front gardens have disappeared, sacrificed for extra parking. Most of the older shops have been replaced by estate agents, coffee bars and fast food places. Ye Gods, how many takeaway chicken places does one road really need? The little Cafe looks pretty low key and tasteful amongst the blousy bright reds and oranges of the chicken shacks and curry houses.

A five minute gap should do the trick, so better make my way back towards the target.

Perusing the outside menu gives an opportunity to suss out where he is sitting. Kaz hasn't arrived yet but I can see that he's preoccupied again with his phone, so he doesn't notice me grabbing the nearest table – discreet but still giving a good observation point. Police jargon I know but it is easy to revert to old habits in these situations. Not that I've done much following on foot lately, but needs must in this case.

I'm still pretending to examine at the menu when Kaz makes her entrance, tall, immaculately dressed in a cream trouser suit that is exquisitely cut. She's slim with her black short hair cut in what my hairdresser would call a 'choppy bob'. Like Steve she's sporting a deep tan but hers looks more natural, one got from a holiday rather than a tanning salon. Pretty too, with barely any makeup – just a slick of lip gloss and a little eye liner.

'Hey Kaz – you look great.' Steve is on his feet and they exchange kisses. These are not the casual peck on the cheek type kisses. If anything they are far more intimate than the ones he gave his partner, Annie Chestnut, earlier on.

'You too Trevor – love the jacket.' She's running her finger along his sleeve, stopping to examine the stitching. Her use of his real name throws me – he's definitely more of a Steve than a Trevor. Jeez, that's an old fashioned name for someone so young.

She glances around the cafe before sitting down. Steve – I'm sticking to my own moniker for him – looking on fondly.

What's the story here I wonder? A work colleague he has a bit of crush on? Old flame? Mistress?

'What can I get you madam?' The waiter's words make me jump and he apologises for taking me unawares. My forced smile tells him that he is forgiven.

'Oh – a coffee please, black, no milk or sugar. And one of those custard tarts as well.'

He nods, making his way back towards the serving area, stopping first to check if Steve and Kaz are ready to order.

It doesn't take them long to decide, both opting for cappuccino coffees, with Kaz choosing sour dough toast topped with avocado. He goes for a full English breakfast with extra bacon. Seems a strange choice for someone so athletic looking but I guess he's planning to hit the gym later.

'So have you told her yet?' Kaz asks after their orders are placed.

A pause from Steve, slight dip of the head.

'No. I nearly did last night but she said she wasn't feeling too well. She's taken the day off to go to the doctors.'

My coffee and custard tart arrives, so I miss the first bit of Kaz's reply. Her expression has changed though, and if I'm not mistaken, she looks irritated.

'You'll have to do it soon Trevor. We can't go on like this, ducking and diving.'

He nods, moving his hand across the table.

'I know Kaz. But the time has to be right. It won't be long now, promise.'

He's trying to placate but it isn't working.

Ah, an affair then? Of course I can't be sure – they could be planning something else entirely – but it isn't looking that innocent. Their words, body language, obvious affection, intimacy of their greetings. No not at all innocent.

Screeching sounds from the coffee machine drown out their next exchange but afterwards she looks more cheerful, flicking back her hair and touching his arm.

If I'm right, poor Annie Chestnut could be in for a shock. That's why she wasn't in her usual work garb this morning, assuming it is her who has the doctor appointment.

I've walked in those shoes too, my long term partner of 20 years, ditching me for – wait for it – another man. Yes, repeat 'man'. Truth be told, things would have been hell of a lot simpler if it had been another woman. We'd already grown apart, just ambling along, my compulsive behaviour worsening as the relationship started to fall apart. In the end, his leaving was no surprise but the choice of new partner was. Our friend, neighbour, and his bloody golfing buddy. When he told me, he used the word 'bi-sexual' – 'it's just one of those things Julie, it's how I'm made' – but that didn't make things any easier. Afterwards, I tried to fathom it out but failed. How could I, a former police officer, have missed the signs?

Juggling two breakfast plates and a side of extra bacon rashers, the waiter's steps gingerly across the floor, face rigid with concentration.

'Here, let me help you with that mate' Steve offers, relieving him of the additional plate. Showing a thoughtful side then, a well brought up young man.

Neither of them say much as they dig into their breakfasts, me trying to eke out my coffee and tart, waiting for another clue as to what is really going on.

It's Kaz who breaks the silence, pushing her plate aside, checking her watch.

'Listen I'm going to have to dash back – I've got to prepare for my staff meeting. You will tell her tonight then?'

Wiping a paper napkin across his lips, Steve nods, leaning across to take her hand.

'Promise I will. I'll ring you later. Here let me sort this, you just get going.' Another kiss, as affectionate as the last, delicate and lingering. In the throes of their goodbye clinch, I manage to grab a photo on my phone. Evidence is everything and I wish someone had done the same for me when my other half was getting up to his tricks.

Decision time then. Hang around while Steve finishes the remnants of his breakfast, or pay up and jump on the next Number 11 heading back towards home, again passing house number 56, the supposed love nest?

The return bus trip has it and leaves plenty of time to update my notes on the journey. Arriving upstairs my favourite seat is already taken damn it, but I manage to bag a clear space further up front.

What to do next about Annie Chestnut then? If her boyfriend is up to something, she needs a warning, a heads up.

As the bus pulls up opposite number 56, I can see

her in the sitting room, dressed now, watching morning TV.

There's just enough time to hop off, apologising to the driver as he is about to close the door. He glares, annoyed that he's got to re-open it, doubtless one of the many irritations of his day.

From pavement level the house seems much bigger, the driveway more imposing than viewed from above. I'll hang around until Annie leaves for her doctor appointment, and then get a better look around.

Already I can see there is one of those wall mounted letter boxes by the front gate – always a good thing - and from where I'm standing there are no obvious signs of security cameras.

Think I will put in a quick call to Renee, my house keeper, who should have got to my place by now. She's been with me since the stabbing incident, the day that tore my world apart.

Renee doesn't take long to answer and I can hear her favourite radio station in the background.

'Morning Renee how are things today?'

Already she's gabbling on about needing more cleaning products and how she'll pop out later to the local store.

'Tell you what Renee,' I interrupt, keeping my eye out for any signs that Annie is on the move. 'We'll go out shopping for stuff together this time. shouldn't be too long.'

'Er...ok Julie. When were you thinking?' I know why she's asking, as it's her day to visit the local swimming pool and like me, Renee is a creature of habit. That's why we've lasted so long, her loyalty and willingness to accept my behaviours. She's not the sharpest knife in the drawer either, so incapable of over thinking. Yes, Renee is the perfect house keeper, totally trustworthy and willing to do as I ask.

I end the call abruptly as Annie Chestnut emerges from the house, wearing a striking pea green coat. She heads off on foot, straight backed and purposeful. I keep watch as she works her way up the street, stepping aside to let a dog walker past, exchanging a few words with him while patting the scruffy looking mutt on the head.

As the green coat disappears into the distance, I make my move, casually crossing the road to inspect the house closer up. It's handy that the outer circle bus stop is right outside, and even better that no-one is waiting there yet. It won't be long before people start to arrive for the next number 11, so first a close-up look at that letter box. Yes, it will be easy to pop something inside without looking suspicious – knowing the bus timetables by heart helps as things can be planned around waiting passengers.

I'm right about the lack of security cameras but always best to play safe at ground level, to do a proper 'recce' as I still like to call it.

Already a plan is hatching on how to warn Annie about her cheating boyfriend. A printed copy of my phone photograph showing them in an intimate clinch – no digital copy for the tech cops to work on if it should come to that – with a note produced on an old typewriter I have squirreled away. I'll make sure nothing can be traced back to me, including any pesky finger print evidence. Yes, once a cop....

Old Mr T's house, the other one I'm keeping a watch on, will have to wait for today. Getting involved in his life should be a lot easier. Just a knock on the door, a question about his cat, has it gone missing? If, so I might have seen it earlier. That kind of thing.

It never fails to surprise me how easy it is to do this and yes, I've done it many times before. Usually it's for the good of the person, helping them out, befriending the lonely. I think Mr T will experience the caring Julie, the one who phones them, takes them out for shopping trips, making herself indispensable.

Time to put in another call to my house keeper and I need her to type up a note. She's used to this and knows the score. The typewriter, the paper I keep in the top desk drawer, the forensic gloves to handle the correspondence and envelope.

'Ok Renee – ready to take this down?'

Her typing is plodding, one fingered. No problem as it gives me time to think.

'Hello from a friend. If it were me this was happening to, I'd want to know. So here's a little photo I took earlier.'

When she's finished typing I instruct her to meet me at the supermarket, after she has followed instructions to print off a copy of my photo. A quick shop before heading back to Annie's to drop off the damning message in her post box. Another life entered into, putting a bombshell at the centre of her universe.

Come on, who wouldn't want to be told in a situation like this? I've never spoken to Annie but I can sense she's a decent person, unlike her rat of a partner. Call it a copper's nose, a sixth sense if you like.

....

The morning after. Same bus, my usual seat, a tin of cat food to deliver to old Mr T. It will be used later as bait to lure back his cat - that's my story anyway. Meantime we might share some tea and toast, get to know each other like I normally do with my chosen clients. After that it's down to me. Do I like them, think I should be a force for good? Or do I go the opposite way, maybe giving them a punishment they deserve - a bit of financial fraud, a burglary? In one case I even helped an awful man enter into the next world - a 'natural' death of course.

First though, an early stop off at Annie's place to check out what is happening. There's no sign of Steve, aka Trevor, or his car. Annie though is back in her work uniform and staring out of the window. From where I'm standing – a strategic few feet from the bus stop – she looks tired, red eyed, distracted.

Then the front door opening, her speedy stride across the garden, face visible close-up. Instinctively I glance down at my phone, trying to look preoccupied, one of the good things about mobile devices.

Is Annie heading off to meet someone? She's stopped by the gate, staring into the middle distance, as if in another world. If I'm not mistaken, a hellish one too.

One smile won't hurt, quick hello just to be sociable.

'You waiting for the next number 11?' I ask giving my well practised and friendliest beam.

She stares across, at first unsmiling and then a flicker on the lower lip. Not a smile but a quiver, my simple interaction being too much.

'Are you alright my dear?'

And that is all it takes. Tears cascade down her cheeks, my comforting words and then the offer – from her – for me to join her on the other side of the gate.

Her tale comes tumbling out, discordant. A sister-in-law who has cancer and it is terminal. She's only just found out in the most horrific of ways. Some-one ('can you believe this?') left a note and a photograph in her letter box. They thought Trevor –

'my fiancé' – was having an affair because he and his sister Kaz had met up in some cafe. They're close you see and probably even more so since she had this news.

'They were keeping it from me' she adds, as I try to hide my shock.

'What I don't understand though, is why someone would put that vile note in my post box. I mean, what sort of sicko does that eh?'

I'm listening – boy I'm listening – and that is all she wants for now.

When I do get my words out, I manage to sound empathetic, sympathetic even.

'Tear it up – go on. Destroy it. Don't let that er, sicko, get to you. At least you know now but don't let them win.'

A pause and I can see that my words are working.

'Come on I'll help you do it. What did you say your name was again?'

'Freya – and yours?'

' Julie'.

She's clinging onto the note and the picture that tells a different story from the one I'd assumed.

'Let's just burn it Ann.. er I mean Freya. Get rid of it for good'.

And with that we head towards the house.

To make a fire. Destroy the evidence. Help is at hand from ace cop Julie.

Me getting involved to put things right again...

We watch as the cooker flames lick the paper, curling, blackening, my arm pressed against Freya's shoulder.

'Now doesn't that feel better?' I ask in my police cum therapist voice.

Her words ring out. 'Thank you. I can't believe I've told you all of this, a complete stranger, but we've done the right thing haven't we?'

My smile is beatific, calming. God only knows there has been enough practice at this sort of thing

'Of course we have.'

Freya, number 21 on my list and counting.

A new relationship about to unfold, heading in whatever direction I chose to take it.

Julie, you see, is always in the driving seat, just like in the old days.

Yes, forever a copper....

Unravelling Freddie

They call us the 'Eleanor' squad,' named after the song about a lonely woman who was anonymous in life and death.

An exquisite first name but who was the real person behind it?

When Eleanor in the song was laid to rest, nobody turned up apart from the priest. Just another hidden life, slipping away unnoticed every single day.

That's where we come in.

Our squad is a team of three investigators, employed by the local council to put a life portrait to the loneliest of passings. Everyone has a life story and - if they were lucky – would have known love too. It is just detective work, piecing together clues, and no coincidence that we are a mix of former police workers and private investigators, happy to use our skills to give some dignity in death.

Dignity.

A small yet important word.

Today the name at the top of my folder is Freddie Mullins. Eighty years old and found in his Nottingham flat after neighbours noticed a build-up of post in his letter box.

The document inside has my title at the top. Anne Cassidy, lone death inspector or LDI to use the acronym. Four decades younger than Freddie, maybe the same age as his children, assuming he has any.

Estimated time of death was about two months before he was discovered, slumped on the sofa, television still on and the remnants of his last supper mouldering nearby.

Most people think it is a depressing job but trust me it isn't. The sense of satisfaction gained when a long lost relative is discovered, the fascinating details unearthed, these are what makes it a privilege. Hand on heart I love what I do, not that most people believe me, preferring to change the subject if it happens to come up.

Freddie's flat has been cleaned but that tell-tale smell still lingers, a sort of sickly sweetness mixed with something else, acrid and pungent. There is an indent in the sofa and a reddish tinge, Freddie's final mark, the detritus of life.

I've got an hour to look around, to take away any items that give a clue to who this man was. None of the neighbours recall seeing any visitors. There were occasional glimpses of Freddie, huddled inside his heavy overcoat whatever the weather, but he never spoke or acknowledged greetings. So everyone stopped trying, accepting him as someone who wanted to be private.

With his overcoat still hanging on the door where he left it, a quick search of the pockets reveals nothing but a part eaten packet of mints. It's a good quality coat though, the checked pattern still visible under the layers of grime. It would have cost a bit back in the day and must have meant something if he wore it so often, a sort of comfort blanket, shield against the outside world.

Bagging up the coat for a more detailed search later, a cursory scan of his post gives little away. There is only one framed photo, which could be Freddie as a younger man, tall, neatly cut black hair and a lopsided grin. A woman is standing beside him, a slender red head with her head bowed shyly. His wife? Girlfriend? The pose is intimate, him leaning towards her, his arm resting on her shoulder. Looking at their clothes I'm guessing it was taken in the early sixties but there is no tell-tale clue on the back of the photo or its frame.

His bookshelf shows a taste for travel, with guide books for France, Italy, Portugal and the former Yugoslavia . An inscription inside one of the French guides reads:

'To Darling Freddie. Here's to more French adventures! Much Love Daphne. Christmas 1966'

A name to go on and perhaps Daphne is the woman in the photo. Strange though, that he had such an interest in travelling but appears to have little in the way of mementoes.

Adding the signed book to my evidence bag, I spot a dusty brown suitcase wedged under the bottom shelf. Using my trusty pen knife to crack open the lock, it is full of old VHS tapes which could reveal vital clues.

Aside from a few clothes, two pairs of well worn shoes and a thread-bare dressing gown strewn across the old style candlewick bed cover, there is little to show for the past thirty years of Freddie's life in this pokey flat. Even by my past experiences of frugal living, this is up there with a lack of personal possessions. I can't help noticing that the furniture – sofa, rickety bookshelf, dressing table and even the bed – is of decent quality. Sign of a once prosperous life?

I'm pretty much finished when my phones rings and it's my colleague, Dave. A few years older than me, he has just joined the squad having retired from the local police.

'How's it going Anne?' he asks, sounding his usual chirpy self.

'Bit thin this one' I reply, eyeing my paltry stash.

'Never mind hon. You up for that drink and catch-up later?'

Damn, I'd clean forgotten, mumbling an excuse about needing to look at Freddie's old films for clues.

'Thought you didn't have much? Why don't I grab a pizza and we can watch together, two lots of eyes are better.'

A deal then, dinner sorted and a trawl through some old footage. Hardly a glamorous evening but I do love an old movie and can pretend it's not really work.

When Dave turns up, he's brandishing a bottle of wine along with a four cheese pizza and a soft drink because he's driving. His former sniffer dog, Barney, is with him – a roan cocker spaniel whose tail never seems to stop wagging.

'Don't mind Barney do you?' he asks, knowing it is a rhetorical question. Barney is looking up with his soft but intelligent eyes and resistance is futile.

The pizza is delicious, the wine less so, being a cheap supermarket plonk. Time then to fire up the VHS player, a relic from my student days.

'Jeez that brings back some memories' Dave jokes as we put in the first tape.

Freddie was no film director, the shots jerky and out of focus. There's no editorial eye either, with footage of pretty Italian towns spliced in with rural Yugoslavia, red roofed houses dotted around the lush hillsides. The woman in the photo I retrieved earlier is in there, always smiling, in summer dresses and kitten heels. So far Freddie is out of shot, preferring to observe rather than make an appearance.

'How do you know it is him filming?' Dave asks,

taking a noisy swig from his drink can.

He's right. This could have been shot by anyone but somehow I think it is the young Freddie lurking behind the camera.

We have moved on to the second tape, this time in 1960s France, when Barney decides to stretch his legs, making a bee-line for my evidence bag.

'Leave' Dave commands, gesturing Barney towards him. Sitting bolt upright, Barney is staring at my bag, fixated.

'Anne there's something bothering him. Mind if I take a look?'

Pausing the tape, he reaches over, grabbing the bag, Barney sticking to his rigid pose.

Carefully taking out Freddie's dressing gown and blanket, he passes them across to Barney who sniffs furiously, his tail swinging side-to-side like a metronome.

Next up the bulky coat, musty smell enveloping my room. Barney circles it, intrigued, exploring with his well trained nose before sitting down beside it, staring back at Dave.

'He's trying to tell us something Anne. Hand me the coat and we'll have a root around'.

While I'm going through the pockets again, Dave is patting around the hemline.

'OK to pull up the lining?' Another rhetorical question as he has already started to tug at the stitching.

We both flinch as a paper package lands on the floor, an elastic band wrapped around the middle.

'There's more' Dave mutters, his hand disappearing deeper into the coat lining.

In all there are six brown paper packets, secured tightly with identical red elastic ties, and another white envelope with the hand written words 'Last Will and Testament'.

That's what made Freddie's old coat so heavy then. Money and lots of it, each package containing £1,000 made up of £20 notes, secreted neatly inside.

Dave hands over the white envelope without taking his eyes off the mound of cash strewn around us.

Inside there is a note written on old style jotter book paper. It is dated July 20 1995 and the handwriting is small, yet controlled.

"To whoever finds this consider it to be my final Will. The £6,000 is yours to keep. I only ask that you do some good with it, something that brings joy. Yours sincerely, Freddie Mullins. "

There is a spidery witness signature underneath. A Mr John Mason, whoever that is - or was.

Neither of us says anything as we stare at the note, Barney guarding the stash as if his life depended on it.

'We should ring the office for advice' I whisper

breaking the silence, a hushed tone somehow feeling appropriate.

Dave doesn't reply, still staring at the pile of money, head shaking in disbelief.

As I'm reaching for the phone, he grabs my arm, his grip taking me by surprise.

'Hang on Anne, let's think this through first.'

Think through? Come on, we both know the score. Any valuables or money found must be photographed and reported straight away. The Eleanor Squad rules are clear.

Yet we've never come across anything like this before, saying that finders are keepers. Dave says that we should sleep on it, report in tomorrow but write down exactly what we did tonight and document everything.

It is gone midnight before we've finished recording the evidence.

'Tell me Anne, if we get to keep this, what would you do with your share?'

I can tell he's excited, probably planning a hi-tech gizmo or a new car.

Me? If it gets to that point, I'd like to go back to those places Freddie visited, stand in the very spots where he took those photos. Find out who the real man was.

After Dave has gone, it is impossible to sleep so I dig out a few more of the Freddie tapes. This time he is grinning at the camera, in front of the lens rather than behind it. He's handsome, in his prime, black hair greased to an inch of its life as was the fashion back then.

There is sound too, unlike the others we viewed. For the first time I hear Freddie's voice with a hint of a northern accent.

'Heh Daph – take a look over there'.

The camera pans to the right towards a group of men singing loudly in a nearby bar, wearing T-shirts marked 'World Cup Willy'. It is Calais in France and it is not long after England won the 1966 football World Cup. The calendar behind the bar, assuming it is right, shows August 15 1966.

They're hollering along to the song 'Yellow Submarine', belting out the chorus.

When the camera pans back, Freddie is grinning and he winks knowingly.

Prescience – a gesture with significance decades down the line?

Then it occurs to me. Bolt out of the blue.

That song, the one our squad is named after.

It was riding high in the music charts on the very day Freddie laughed and winked at the camera. Yes, a double-sided release with a song about a yellow submarine

Right now Freddie is staring back at me, dark eyes playful, teasing.

An eerie coincidence which is both intriguing and poignant.

A small moment frozen in time,

All those years ago.

Deadline

Tick. Tock.

How long have we really got?

I mean *'really'*, in the full sense of the word.

Assuming bad health, a crime or accident doesn't take us away first, should we all bow out at an agreed age? Celebrate our lives with a big joyous send off, and then simply – yes simply - call it a day.

Not so much raging against the dying of the light, but partying into it, raving if you like.

Admittedly, not the questions most people have to mull over while sipping their first morning cappuccino, but hey, this is my job.

The official title is 'adviser' to the new 'Think The Unthinkable' group, a motley collection of health professionals pulled together to do some blue sky pondering. We're here to shake, rattle and roll conventional thinking, turn over established practices, and give them a good kick about

'Sounds like a waste of tax payer's money,' my dad scoffed when I told him about my new job. 'I mean what the hell will you do all day?'

'Just think dad. That's the whole point.'

Not that he'd appreciate the importance of flexing brain muscles, only understanding work as something you can touch or feel at the end of the day.

Words peer out from a note headed 'Urgent - Need Your Thoughts Pronto.'

There's a PS too. Isn't there always?

'Ideas are needed by 12pm in time for a pow-wow with the Minister'.

Even by Steve Baxter's standards, this is a short missive, which means it's quite important. Steve, the boss who only minces words when he's relaxed or tipsy on red wine and whisky chasers.

To be fair, he's got every right to feel the need to down several bottles a day. Heading up the Government's controversial Think-A-Thon, Stevie boy has his work cut out.

Enough about him though and a bit about yours truly.

Trish Cunningham. Writer for a health magazine, the sort that only gets read by a few policy makers, and even fewer interested professionals. Mum of one, and back shacking up with my folks until the divorce gets settled.

At this crossroads in my life, self-pitying and broke, I got a surprise call from Steve,

'What's the catch?' I asked, when he offered to triple my salary and swap my stressful, under-paid post for something that seemed just too good to be true.

'None. We just want to pick that specialist brain of yours.'

Fast forward six months, and here I am in a pristine new City of London office with a view across to St Paul's Cathedral, looking more like a trendy dot.com business than an off-shoot of central government. Me, and the rest of the six strong team have our own separate 'work pods', the complete opposite of my old messy and noisy open plan office. Not a piece of paper in sight, desk toys or anything personal frowned upon. Silent, clinical, soulless.

My remit is end of life, the most controversial area of the lot, as Steve keeps reminding me.

His mantra, 'Crack this one Trish and you'll be the star of the show,' is his way of encouraging me to come up with some big bold ideas for change. Something to get the mandarins and MPs jumping up from their comfortable, well fed backsides.

By the way, that description is in 'Steve speak', but you get the idea.

Right, better get a move on if I'm to get this latest task done in time. First, the need to come up with a hypothetical age that most people would agree is an acceptable time to depart their human form. That's tricky because the older you get the more you're going to push the off-button forwards. When you're in your twenties you think sixty is ancient, but after hitting forty, as I did a year ago, the big '60' doesn't seem that far away.

This could be one to run past Mum, now in her mid sixties. She'll be fine to talk now, back home from dropping my daughter Ellie off at school.

Mum sounds out of breath when she eventually answers the phone.

'Sorry I was just getting the post. Why are you ringing at this time anyway?'

I wait as she gets her breath back.

'Mum, I haven't got long but I just need to check something with you.'

'OK but you're not the only one in a rush. I don't want to miss Pop Quiz on the radio.' Good old mum, ever the creature of habit.

Straight to the point then.

'This might sound odd, but what age do you think most people would want to die if they really had the choice? 80? 85?'

No answer for what seems a long time and then the sharp intake of breath, meaning disapproval.

'Bloody hell Trish, you do come out with some rubbish. Is this what they pay you to do, float daft questions like that?' Yet another huff to reinforce her point.

'Come on Mum...humour me'

'Well if I have to play this ridiculous game, I'd go for around 85 and remind you that would give me and your dad another twenty years. Enough to see little Ellie graduate and maybe walk down the aisle.'

Hell, talk about bringing things right down to the personal. My little girl would be 30 by then, maybe even with children of her own. Still, we're accentuating the positive here, having a deadline for your life so that your older years are more comfortable, that you don't slide into even poorer health and eventual senility.

Of course, that fate doesn't apply to everyone over 85, but a line has to be drawn somewhere and for now it will do.

Come to think of it, both my sets of grandparents disappeared well before their eightieth birthdays, and I only have the haziest recollection of them. Grandpa Cunningham, who lost part of a finger while working in the Docks and used it to stub down his pipe tobacco, the truncated end as brown as a conker. His stories about how he came to lose the digit, with each one differing from the last. For me that didn't matter, I just loved those tales as much as grannie Cunningham's butterfly cakes. As for the other set, mum's parents, they retired to Devon and only came up to London once a year. We never did get to see them in their sea-side idyll, but I remember their photos of palm trees in the garden, the boxes of fudge, and how skinny my number two grandpa had got on what turned out to be their last visit.

Fleeting memories, occasionally made fresh by digging out faded photographs.

A quick goodbye to mum and then the task in hand.

It doesn't take long for the figures to bounce onto my screen. If we plan that the vast majority of us depart in our mid eighties, generous pensions can be paid to everyone once they turn sixty. Social and health care will improve, with billions more to spend on making later lives more enjoyable.

If you can believe the number crunching there are lots of pros, and let's be honest here, wouldn't life become more meaningful if we had a clear leaving date? We could stop pretending that we'll go on forever - the biggest con in the modern world - and instead focus on living better.

A screech is followed laughter. Soft running, unmistakably child-like and then playful whoops.

Enough of a distraction to drag me away from graphs and figures, to follow the sound.

There's a toddler, I'm guessing about two years old, in a garish orange coat which is way too big. Nearby is an elderly man, maybe the child's grandpa, grappling with a carrier bag, chasing after the tot who sees it all as a wonderful game.

The man is going along with it, pretending that the youngster is too fast to catch. Moving closer, and then dropping back, the child's laughter getting louder, joyous, a symphony of play.

Transfixed, I edge closer to the window to get a better look. The youngster rolling on the grassy verge, a tangle of orange with a wayward mop of brown hair. The man now sitting down, rummaging in the bag, and gesticulating to the child.

He's shouting something but the child is oblivious, intent on continuing the game.

My phone rings out. Damn. I'm reluctant to answer it, wanting to see how the man coaxes the mischievous tot to come back to him.

A quick glance shows that it's Steve, so better respond.

'Trish - how's it going?' He's straight in there before I can even say hello

Brain wrenched into gear, a desperate attempt to sound upbeat.

'Oh not bad. I've got an age to play with, 85, and the numbers look good. The pros are easy but I'm just about to start on the hard bit.'

He pauses, mulling over my words.

'Just keep an eye on the clock Trish, and all being well that gives me another twenty five years. I think I can live with that.'

Then he's gone, no little niceties like 'goodbye' or 'catch up later.'

In the real world, the man and child are sitting together, sharing some food from the carrier bag. Wordless, fixated on whatever snack they are eating.

Before heading back to the computer, I need some fresh air, to clear my head before taking on the really big question, the one dealing with enforcement. Let's be clear about this, if the dying at 85 policy is to work, then there has to be some real persuasion. Plenty of things to make it attractive, but genuine penalties for any change of mind.

'Penalties'. A word with huge consequences.

Despite the mid morning sunshine it is cold, and stupidly I've ventured out without a jacket. Up close, I can see that the man looks much older, his sprightly play belying his age. He's wiping the remains of a yoghurt pot from the child's jacket, streaks of the sticky pinkish gunk trickling down the sleeve.

'Do you need a wet wipe?' I ask, at the same time reaching into my bag to retrieve a pack.

The man smiles, thanking me, accepting my gift and gently admonishing his charge for being a messy boy. Ah, a boy then, and after wiping the jacket clean, he introduces me to his 'great grandson' Nathan.

A lovely name and my earlier guess was right, he's two years old. I remember Ellie at that age and it was hard work, a mix of infant and emerging little person with a will of their own.

I discover that the man is called Howard, and he's looking after his great grandson because the parents are visiting Poland for a few days.

'A holiday?' I ask, pulling across my woefully inadequate cardigan for warmth.

'Not really'. The man looks sad, staring hard at the boy.

'They're actually visiting Auschwitz, where most of my family died. It's a trip they've been meaning to take for ages'.

God, what to say?

Stay silent, a universal mark of sorrow and respect.

'I was one of the lucky ones. Got out just in time and arrived safely in London.' He's still staring at the boy, as if he can't quite believe he's really here.

The voice is pure East End London, not a trace of his original accent. Strong, unfaltering, confident even.

Another pause, as I think about the young Howard, snatched away from everything he loves, thrown into a strange new world, disconnected to save his life.

'Can you believe Trish, I'll be ninety three on my next birthday? Not a bad innings, eh?' He's smiling again, the sadness gone, eyes lit up, sparkly, playful.

He scoops up little Nathan, planting a kiss on his cheek.

'Now say thank you to the kind lady.'

Nathan grins shyly, handing me his yoghurt pot. Same eyes as his great grand daddy, no mistaking the heritage.

'I'd better get back to work ' I reply, ruffling Nathan's hair, passing back the half eaten present.

'What do you do for a living Trish?' Howard isn't quite ready to end our conversation, not without a clue to who I am, what I'm about.

Right now I could kick myself for even mentioning work.

'Oh - it's a sort of civil service type job. You know, brings in the money'

He's staring hard at me, no doubt sensing that I'm not telling the whole truth and must have my reasons for doing so.

'Well goodbye Trish and thanks again for your help. Hope you have a long and happy life, just like me.'

His handshake is firm, the skin soft, warmer than expected. They walk away, hand-in-hand, me unable to move, eyes hot, and fighting back tears.

For what? A complete stranger's story?

There have been so many over the years, told to me in my work as a journalist. People trusting me to put their lives into the public domain, tell their stories and help bring about change.

My role to remain detached, not to get too involved. The trick of the observer, the recorder for posterity and a way to stay sane.

Returning to my clinical work station, the list of

pros for death at 85 is dancing before my eyes.

Arguments against then...

A). People will naturally want to delay their departure as it approaches. To push forward the fateful day. Rage, rage.

'Howard'.

B). Loved ones would try to stop it, to cling on to their cherished family and friends.

'Nathan'.

C).For an agreed cut-off age to work, there would have to be huge rewards for consent, and effective 'punishment' for failing to go ahead. The carrot is easy - but an acceptable stick?

'Howard. Nathan. Howard. Nathan'.

Damn it, their names are dancing in my brain. Slowly at first, building to a crescendo. Frantic, stomping, screaming.

Enough.

In this brave new actuarial world, their relationship wouldn't even exist. Howard already dead, Nathan without his much loved great grandpa.

Howard having lived through tragedy, with so much still to give, spirited away earlier for the supposed greater good. Disposable and a convenient calculation to make the number crunchers and policy strategists happier.

Tick-tock.

Tick-boxes, pluses and minuses.

Life is a glorious messy affair and shouldn't we leave it that way?

The clock shows fifteen minutes to go before my policy prophecies are needed. Fingers hovering over the key board like a pianist about to play.

One.

'Howard'.

Two.

'Nathan'.

Three...

Are you sure you want to delete? The computer warning flashes before my eyes. Accusatory, the nanny of the digital world.

A deep breath and...

Delete, delete, delete.

Blank screen, followed by the departmental logo 'Think The Unthinkable' snaking across the monitor, mocking, goading.

Just for once in my one and only life.

A deadline missed.

Two Doors

There can't be many people who have been dubbed 'The Nation's Most Hated Woman'.

The headline is there for eternity, peering out from the screen every time I search out my name. My old name that is.

Today I'm called Kirsty, Ms K Smith, and yes, the second bit was chosen deliberately. Commonplace and buried deeply amongst the millions of Smiths already out there. 'Kirsty', because I've always liked the name, with its nod to the Scottish side of the family.

What's in a name? As things go, everything.

The new me lives in a seaside town in deepest West Cornwall, the end of the line, next step the Atlantic Ocean. It's the pole opposite of south London, the place I used to call home, but an easy place to go under the radar. 'Carol Potter', the person who used to be me, is to all intents and purposes dead, gone forever courtesy of deed poll. At least as far as the wider world is concerned.

Still, that headline from three years ago, lives on, goading, mocking, censorious. The woman who used to be me did wrong, made a professional call that led to a tragedy.

If only this, if only that.

If only.

My best friend Tim, one of a handful of trusted people I'm still in touch with, gives well meaning advice. 'That was then, this is now,' is his mantra.

As if life was so simple, black or white, left or right.

Which is why now and again, I torture myself by calling up that headline. The social worker, the one who is supposed to protect, to save lives – the 'do-gooder' – has screwed up. Made a wrong call, done bad.

Yes, the nightmare began way back then but is still in the here and now. Every day and night, the jabbing question 'what if?'

What if I'd waited for an extra half hour, after my knock on the door was ignored?

What if I'd called the police, to get them to force entry?

And the muffled cry, the one that seemed to come from deep inside the drab pebble dashed walls. Should I have listened harder, stood my ground?

Questions, questions, in a relentless loop.

On that fateful day, it was the closest of calls, the next family on my list a young girl just placed with a new foster family. She wasn't settling well and the tension in the foster mum's voice was palpable.

'Carol, could you call around? I need to talk. *Please...*'

Yet this visit was urgent too. I hadn't seen the young lad inside for two weeks. There was concern about how his parents were coping, reports of shouting, crying.

On my last few house calls he seemed well cared for and nourished, but that can be misleading.

Every good child protection worker knows to look beyond the obvious, the superficially OK. It takes time and co-operation.

Time, the devil's currency, with never enough to go around, ticking away, speeding off just when you think you've caught up.

Right now time was of the essence and the decision was a fine one.

Prioritise this youngster or go to the struggling foster mum?

Heads you win.

Tails you...

Spinning an imaginary coin, I set off to the foster home.

Next the nightmare call in the early hours, my supervisor's voice cracked and panicked.

The boy, the one whose house I sat outside only a few hours before, was missing. Police already scouring CCTV, calls to the public to look out for a vulnerable 9 year old boy.

Another terrible phone call followed, the worst kind, one you never want to hear. A boy found in a park lake, with no doubt about the identity.

'Carol - why didn't you just stay put until you could get into the house?'

Of course I knew why my supervisor had to ask this, the question that still haunts in the wee small hours.

The headlines followed quickly, a clamour for a full inquiry, blame and shame because an innocent life had been lost.

Abject failure by those whose duty it was to protect. Could have done. Should have done. Yes, some responsibility could be placed with the family but an incompetent so-called 'professional' too.

In the court of popular opinion, I deserved everything I got and in the end there was no choice but to scurry away. Of course, well meaning friends and family begged me to lie low, to ride the storm.

'This too will pass'.

Well pass it didn't and in the end there was only one solution if you can really call it that. A complete change of identity, move to a place where no one knew me. Not a soul.

'Mum – must you really go?' My son's voice cuts

in as I pack up my belongings on the bleakest of February mornings.

His answer is written in my face, cheek bones jutting out from several stones in weight loss, eyes pink from sleeplessness.

'I wish dad was still here for you' he adds, knowing there is no point in trying to stop this madness of mine.

'So do I son'. My words jump out, mechanical, clipped, no sign of the emotions raging inside.

God, I wish I could go back to that time when my world seemed perfect. With an adored husband and a son who didn't have to learn the hard way that the world can be the cruellest of places.

But to quote my best mate again, 'that was then'. A life before being widowed way too early, left behind with a grown-up son still angry that his dad had gone. Before making a tragic professional mistake, and being forced to flee to a remote part of the country.

'I'll visit as much as I can' he says, and I know he means it. Yet we both understand that this will only be the occasional week or so worked around his busy job in the city.

Here I am then. Today is what the Cornish call 'mizzly', a mix of soft rain and low level sea mist. My small terraced house, or sea-side 'cottage' as the estate agent calls it, is just a short walk away from my new day job.

This work role wasn't planned. Arriving here with no close friends or family, I had to find a way to get involved in the community before going crazy with loneliness and boredom. After all, there are only so many scenic views you can take in before that holiday feeling wears off, the reality of living a disconnected life hitting hard.

An ad in the local paper jumped out at just the right time.

'Volunteers needed for a new community project aimed at combating social isolation.'

Bingo. Helping others but at the end of a computer, a cyber adviser of sorts. Using my professional skills but in a different, lower profile way.

There was a short interview, if you can even call it that, in a cafe by Newlyn Harbour not far from where I live.

'Tell me a bit about you', the earnest young man asked, hovering over his iPad.

I'd already rehearsed my 'backstory' with a big omission. Years in London as a stay-at-home mum, widowed at the age of just 44 when my husband died, followed by an escape to Newlyn to start a new chapter of my life.

'Sorry to hear about your husband' the young man replied, not a bit of sincerity in his voice. My tale rang true that's the main thing, no more questions asked.

After starting out as a volunteer on-line 'befriender', a few months down the line the project attracted some local funds which led to a part-time wage. It's not much but my needs are small and by focusing on the problems of others, I can get some respite from my own.

Today, there are five emails and one in particular catches my eye.

'Hello Kirsty, I was in touch a few weeks ago about a problem with my neighbour. I did what you said but I need to talk to you about something else. Can you give me a call this time? Cheers. Sally.'

Mostly we are encouraged to stay on-line, with a clear record of our conversations, but can use our discretion on occasional follow-up phone calls.

I can recall the original email which told a tale of a frail woman with a seemingly chaotic life, a house chock full of debris and rotting food, refusing all offers of help from well meaning neighbours.

With my past background, I knew what to advise. Avoid being judgemental, alert the local community services department, and meantime see if she can become a trusted person, a confidante of sorts.

Sally has left her home number and when she answers, her voice throws me. A broad Northern Irish accent, friendly yet wary.

She relaxes once she knows who I am, a quick exchange of pleasantries before we cut to the chase.

'The thing is Kirsty, she won't come to the bloody door. I've tried everything, notes through the letter box, arranging a visit from community services like you said, asking the local vicar to help...' I can hear her exasperation, punctuated by frustrated sighs.

Won't come to the door.

Instantly, I'm back in a dingy south London street, staring at an ugly rust stained pebble dashed wall, another door firmly locked.

Right now my head is yelling at me to 'back off, leave it to the others'. Yet a smaller inner voice is whispering, 'Come on. Do the right thing this time.'

Heads you win...

Half an hour later and I'm standing with Sally outside a modern town house on the edge of Newlyn. At least the outside looks spruce, as does the petite woman standing beside me, a bit younger than I expected.

A quick peep through the door flap reveals an inside which lies in stark contrast to the exterior, with barely space to move, cardboard boxes and discarded food wrappers everywhere. The stench of rotten food, mould and urine attacks my nostrils, a vile gassy mix of decay.

Then the glimpse of a foot, a dislodged shoe, a sock crumpled and laced with holes.

'Sally – what's the woman's name?' I'm already punching in the emergency number on my phone.

'It's Mary. Why – what's up?'

No time to reply, as the operator's voice kicks in.

I'm still trying to show Sally where I've spotted the protruding foot, when the ambulance arrives.

Sally does the talking, the crew trawling through the details of Mary's life.

Their words cascade. Likely fall, given the amount of clutter, suspected stroke but responsive. No known relatives, a neighbour will accompany her to the hospital. Another witness is at the scene.

'Are you willing to give a statement?' one of the crew asks me.

Once again, I'm transported to London, being quizzed about why I hadn't fought harder to get inside what turned out to be a house of horrors.

'No, I'd rather leave that to Sally, she knows her best.'

Sally cuts in, thinking I'm being way too modest.

'But Kirsty, you've probably helped save her life. You didn't have to come over and if you hadn't been here, I doubt I'd have been brave enough to even look through the door.'

Whatever the truth of the matter, I must disappear. Slink back into my anonymity, hidden away, well out of sight.

'You're a bloody hero' Sally insists. 'We should be shouting it from the rooftops.'

No way is that going to happen. My smile is forced, more of a grimace.

Yet for the briefest of times, this hated woman is redeemed.

Until she wakes up in the night, heart pounding, alone in a city street.

A child whimpering.

Unheard.

And the headlines branded onto her brain.

The ones that will never disappear.

Namesakes

People say amazing things happen when you are about to die. That your life flashes before you and that you can look down on yourself from above. They say all of this but as far as I'm concerned none of it is true. Trust me things are not that dramatic, not that exciting. And I should know because I can remember in vivid technicolour what happened as I was about to depart this earth.

The thing is I didn't actually drift away in the end. An army of paramedics and specialist doctors managed to pull me back. Strange that I can recall the exact details of the hours leading up to my near death experience – that is what they call it. *Near death experience*. Sounds so precise, so clinical.

So what do I remember? The boring work meeting that lasted two hours and still nothing got sorted. Funny how that has stuck. The need to get some fresh air and exercise. The yen for a toasted mozzarella and pesto sandwich from Gino's Deli. The cold fresh orange juice that tasted delicious and I can picture myself waving to Dave who runs the corner fruit stall. Everything is brightly coloured, garish like one of those old film posters.

Then the next bit. The piercing screech, the smell of burning rubber, smoke and the feeling of warm liquid around my head as I'm lying on the ground. The sandwich squashed in my hand with a gloopy trickle of mozzarella. After that nothing, zippo, it's all gone. Possibly forever if you can believe the doctors. Not that I have great faith in doctors and I've seen enough of them lately to know what I'm talking about.

Now here's the thing. They say I have temporal lobe damage. To you and me that means a head injury caused when the motor bike crashed into me and left me for dead. It also means that I now live the perfect life if you can believe all those self help books. You know the ones where they say you should live in the present to be truly happy?

Well I'm living in the present all right. Every single day. Ask me what I did yesterday and I won't have a clue. You see my new mind is like a blackboard that gets wiped every day and I start with a fresh brain the next morning. Brilliant. No past, no regrets about what I did yesterday. Just living in the moment.

The other thing I should mention since I've been told it is part of my brain condition. I've developed this nagging need to look up all the people who share my name. It is quite overwhelming. The doctors say it is about me 'trying to reinforce my identity' or some such rubbish. So I've been busy on the internet searching all the other Josie James' out there. That's me by the way or 'JJ' to my friends. Of course there's plenty about yours truly – me the Josie James immortalised in the press cuttings about my accident. Me the brave 'brought back from the brink' Josie who is permanently brain damaged. Me the poor young woman whose life will never be the same. Pass the sick bowl.

Then there is the other Josie clan. My namesakes. They are getting up to a surprising number of fascinating things are my namesakes. It makes for utterly compelling reading. And boy do I need to make copious detailed research notes otherwise I'd have to start again from scratch every day. Each night I print out three copies of the notes and put them in exactly the same place on the table at the side of my bed so I know where they are when I wake up. The doctor keeps asking me why I need three copies. It's just because it makes me feel better stupid.

I've now narrowed things down to the three favourite Josies on my list. All were born within a few years of me so we've got age in common – 30 years more or less. I have this growing compulsion to enter their world and to become a real part of their lives. I see them as my new extended family, something to focus on each day. The doctors talk about obsession being common in brain injured patients. Well they can go to hell. This is my world, my hobby.

So let me introduce you to my on-line family.

New York Josie lives in Greenwich Village. She's

an art teacher and lives on her own with a cat called Kitty. I like that, an obvious cat name but funny. I've told her all about my head injury (I find the sympathy vote works every time) and she tells me that art is great therapy. I should try it. She has already invited me over to New York and I want to go. The doctors insist I'm not in a position to travel without a carer but we'll see.

Then there's Portuguese Josie. She's a chef and lives in Vilamoura with her husband Alberto and two year old twins Paulo and Sofia. Strictly speaking Portuguese Josie is Scottish and originally from Edinburgh. I've also told her about my brain injury and she says a seafood diet could work miracles. She has encouraged me to keep up my diary and says she can't imagine how awful it must be not to recall things from one day to the next. Imagine not remembering your child, your husband or your favourite recipes. She's not invited me over yet but you never know. Her beachside house is stunning and her husband looks well handsome lucky woman.

And now to my favourite namesake. Tralee Josie, or Jo as she likes to be called, lives in the West of Ireland and was a finalist in the 'Rose of Tralee' a sort of beauty (with brains) contest. A fat lot of the good my brain would be if I were to enter. Wouldn't do too well on the looks front now either. Tralee Jo works in a bank and is beautiful in a dark Irish way. She has a boyfriend called Callum who isn't much of a looker in my view. A classic beauty and the beast. She says she is too focussed on her career to settle down yet and is intrigued by my poor injured head. Had I considered going off to Lourdes? An aunt of her was apparently cured of arthritis when she travelled there.

Anyway, back to my list. I think I'd like to begin with Tralee Jo and get further into her life. Let's see where this little adventure takes me.

Note in triplicate for tomorrow. Email Tralee Jo and invite her to visit me here at the brain injury centre. No harm in trying. If doctors bang on about my fixation with my namesakes I'll tell them they've got the wrong end of the stick. I just want to make new friends and get to know about their interesting lives. And what's wrong with that?

....

9am at the brain rehabilitation centre. Dr Peters has just popped in. He asks how the cooking lessons are going. For some reason they think I've got to learn about cooking in readiness for a time when I might be able to move into one of the centre's self contained flats. I reply that I'd love to answer him if I could remember what I actually cooked yesterday. He smiles as I reach for my diary. Ah yes, prawn omelette. I think it tasted OK but couldn't be sure 12 hours down the line. And how was I feeling in myself? What a crap question. How would you feel if you had a motorcycle smash into you with your world as well as your head turned upside down?

Now I've got rid of him I can concentrate on the real point of my day. Time to contact Tralee Jo and to get more involved.

How to start? I'll resort to the sympathy vote. So out with another reference to the 'poorly brain'.

'Hi Jo. It's that other Josie with the bad head. Have just got rid of my doctor who actually asked me how I was feeling! Can you believe that? I told him I was fine apart from the little matter of the mashed brain. He didn't laugh but looked at me as if he wanted to say "ungrateful cow". Which I am of course. Anyway, enough about me. When are you going to get over to London? You mentioned in your last email that you have an aunt in Islington and that you might be coming over to see her? Well you mustn't come over without visiting yours truly in this wonderful 5 star establishment (not). Over to you…JJ x'

It's great how email can just be pinged off and automatically saved in the sent folder for future reference. Genius.

Time now for a cup of coffee and a think about what to do if Tralee Jo gets back to say yes, we can really meet up. Ideally she won't bring that Callum because what I'd really like is a long chat about life and men. Especially men like Mark who used to be my boyfriend until all this happened. Mark who disappeared as soon as he realised that the old me was no more. About how my mum and brother have stopped coming to visit because they get upset when they have to introduce themselves to me every time. Thanks folks. Love you too.

Tralee Jo will be a good listener I know it. She'll be like the pretend sister I used to have as a child and won't ask crass questions. She'll tell me about her time as a beauty queen and about her high flying bank job. I'll hear all about the flat she is buying and she'll give me advice about clothes and make-up.

Hang on. The computer has just pinged.

'Hi JJ. Good to hear from you. Funny you should mention London. Heard that there is a big banking conference in London next month and my boss has said I can go! Chance to see my auntie Kath at the same time. It would be great to meet you in person too. I'll contact you with more details once I have them. Really looking forward to meeting you properly. All the best, Jo x Ps Don't be too hard on your doctor, he's just doing his job.'

Well, well. Here we go. An exciting chance of a new friendship. Must make a note in the diary with my three separate safety copies.

....

Dr Peters has just popped in again to tell me that Tralee Jo has been on the 'phone to him. She has been asking all about me and wants to call back to have a 'proper' chat with me. Yes me. I'm so excited I could burst and I throw my arms around Dr Peters. He steps back and asks me if I'm really OK about talking to a stranger and says that I shouldn't get my hopes up too much. Talk about bursting my bubble the miserable old git. And she's not a stranger. We've been in touch by email loads of times now and I've got my diary to prove it.

It wasn't a long chat in the end but enough for

me to know that Tralee Jo is definitely visiting London on June 11. That's already in the diary. She sounds friendly in a genuine sort of way with a lovely soft Irish accent. She is really interested in the problems I'm having with my memory and is reading up on people who have similar conditions. I like that. A considerate soul.

....

A smell of burning rubber and smoke has hurtled me back to the day of my accident. Again I'm lying on the pavement with the sound of sirens and emergency lights flashing. But then somehow the scene has shifted. Dr Peters is there chatting to a police man and I'm outside the red bricked rehabilitation building. This isn't how it should be. I hear Dr Peters asking me if I'm all right and he's saying something about checks for smoke inhalation. From what I can make out, someone in the centre has broken the rules and has fallen asleep with a lit cigarette. He helps me stand up and all I can see are these huge flames billowing out of the building. Have to go back inside. I need my memory diary, my notes, my computer, my new found family. Dr Peters drags me back and I hear myself letting out a scream before two paramedics propel me towards an ambulance.

Then there is nothing. Just an overwhelming desire to return to a search I believe I must have started. Except now I have absolutely no idea what is it. I'm sitting in a room which looks and smells strange with an odd looking computer, an email log on that I don't recognise and shiny black diary. It has my name on it. Josie James.

A nurse has told me that all my notes have disappeared. But what notes? I've no idea what she's talking about.

The calendar on the wall tells me it's June 1st. A new day and a blank canvas.

Finalist in the 2011 Writers and Artists Short Story Competition

Now that you have read these stories, would you consider writing a review? Reviews are the best way for readers to discover new books and will be much appreciated.

And if you enjoyed the stories then do try my other books. See details and reviews on websites www.maggiefogarty.com and www.amazon.co.uk or www.amazon.com.

About the Author:

Maggie Fogarty is a Royal Television Society award winning television producer and journalist, making TV programmes for all the major UK broadcasters. She has also written extensively for a number of national newspapers and magazines.

'My Bermuda Namesakes' was her debut novel and grew out of the original short story 'Namesakes'. It was written during a year long stay in Bermuda where Maggie's husband, Paul, was working as a digital forensics consultant. During her time on the island, Maggie wrote a guest column for the Bermuda Sun newspaper.

She has also written three novellas, 'Dear Mr.DJ', 'Dilemmas and Decisions' and 'Backwards and Forwards'. (The 'Dilemma Novellas' series).

Maggie and her husband live in West Cornwall with their cockapoo dog Bonnie. Before moving there, they lived on the outskirts of Birmingham, in the English Midlands, where Maggie was born and grew up.

Author website: www.maggiefogarty.com

Printed in Great Britain
by Amazon